HEART OF THANKS

Hearts of the Highlands

Paula Quinn

© Copyright 2020 by Paula Quinn
Text by Paula Quinn
Cover by Wicked Smart Designs

Dragonblade Publishing, Inc. is an imprint of Kathryn Le Veque Novels, Inc.
P.O. Box 7968
La Verne CA 91750
ceo@dragonbladepublishing.com

Produced in the United States of America

First Edition July 2020
Print Edition

Reproduction of any kind except where it pertains to short quotes in relation to advertising or promotion is strictly prohibited.

All Rights Reserved.

The characters and events portrayed in this book are fictitious. Any similarity to real persons, living or dead, is purely coincidental and not intended by the author.

ARE YOU SIGNED UP FOR DRAGONBLADE'S BLOG?

You'll get the latest news and information on exclusive giveaways, exclusive excerpts, coming releases, sales, free books, cover reveals and more.

Check out our complete list of authors, too!

No spam, no junk. That's a promise!

Sign Up Here

www.dragonbladepublishing.com

Dearest Reader;

Thank you for your support of a small press. At Dragonblade Publishing, we strive to bring you the highest quality Historical Romance from the some of the best authors in the business. Without your support, there is no 'us', so we sincerely hope you adore these stories and find some new favorite authors along the way.

Happy Reading!

CEO, Dragonblade Publishing

Additional Dragonblade books by Author Paula Quinn

Rulers of the Sky Series
Scorched
Ember
White Hot

Hearts of the Highlands Series
Heart of Ashes
Heart of Shadows
Heart of Stone
Lion Heart
Tempest Heart
Heart of Thanks

Chapter One

Invergarry, Scotland
Christmastide
The Year of Our Lord 1339

E LYSANDE MACPHERSON WALKED into the great hall of the even greater MacPherson stronghold in Invergarry and smiled at the sight before her. With the help of her cousins, they had decorated the hall and just about everywhere else with mountain laurel, fir, and pine with cones attached, and holly branches. The flora was hung on walls and tables, over archways and mantels, and in vases on the tables. Everywhere she went, it smelled like the outdoors and baked goodness from the hall's own kitchen. Delicious wassail warmed the bones and small, rectangular mince pies were handed out to everyone, all prepared with shredded beef, cinnamon, cloves, and nutmeg. Later, they would feast on salmon pottage with carrots, parsnips, and an array of leafy vegetables, clootie dumplings, Christmas cakes, bread puddings and more.

It was Christmas Eve, the beginning of Christmastide for the next twelve days. The celebration was going well. No one had been killed...yet. In fact, everyone seemed to be enjoying the celebration. Even Elysande's slippered foot tapped to the merry music played by her kin.

Her eyes found Cainnech MacPherson amidst the faces. She still considered her father the most handsome of all the men she'd ever seen. He was big and broad-shouldered in his belted plaid. He wore his hair shaved on the sides with the rest braided down his back. His eyes were like shards of sapphire in frost.

He was the only one scowling, staring across the hall at his enemy, Robbie Cameron, who had been invited by Elysande's uncle, Torin, in the hopes of ending their kin's feud.

Peace. It was the talk at every table inside the stronghold—which consisted of three main stone manor houses, several smaller cottages, a great hall with its own kitchen, a gatehouse, a church, several smiths, two tanners, a handful of carpenters and other tradesmen, a garden where much of the food was grown and a wall surrounding all of it.

Everyone had their own opinions on peace. Her father's was that peace could only be achieved when his enemies were dead. She knew his past. She understood why he felt the way he did about many things. She appreciated the measures he went to in order to guarantee her safety, but her father—her dear, loving father was driving her mad. He was also driving all of her suitors away. All. Away.

She was ten and nine and not getting any younger. She wanted a husband and a family, but her father scared everyone away. No matter how far they traveled. He threw them all out and shot arrows at them from the wall. The few he did allow in, he eventually frightened into running, and that was the end of them.

Only Hugh had remained. Hugh Tanner, the son of her father's friend, which meant that he wasn't as hated as all the rest. She found him in the crowd. He was tall and handsome with light blond hair to his shoulders and a bit of sharpness to his nose. She'd resigned herself after her last suitor was tossed out of the stronghold on his arse that

Hugh would likely be the man she married. She wasn't in love with him, but that didn't matter, did it?

His gaze found hers and she smiled, hoping he liked what she wore for the celebration—dark red skirts, a white kirtle and an embroidered, red overcoat and a wreath of mountain laurel in her hair.

But Hugh turned away and went back to listening to another man speak. From where she stood, Elysande couldn't see the man but his voice was like satin across her ears. He spoke of a woman and how he admired her even over the male commanders he had known.

Curious to hear about such a woman, Elysande squeezed her way through the small crowd around him.

When she saw the storyteller, she stopped. He was quite handsome, heart-wrenchingly so. His hair was black and tied at his nape, though some stray strands escaped and fell around his face. His skin was the color of moonlight. He wore a short tunic, belted at the waist. He carried no weapon, as any guests not living at the stronghold were not permitted to bring weapons inside with them. Woolen hose and boots encased his calves and long, muscular thighs. She cleared her throat and blushed, admiring his raw virility. He must have a wife…or several lovers. Even if he didn't, she had her father to get through.

She turned around to see if her father was watching, but she couldn't see him when the crowd closed in, so she returned her attention to the stranger. Was he Cameron's son? There were other welcomed guests attending. Elysande hoped he was one of those.

"I didna arrive until later in the year," said the glorious stranger with pale green eyes wreathed in lush black lashes.

The closer Elysande came to him, the weaker her breath became.

"But as 'twas told to me, the Earl of Dunbar was away and, thinkin' the castle would be an easy target, the English tried to take it. But the castle was under the command of the earl's wife, Lady Agnes Randolf, Countess of Moray—or Black Agnes, as she is known because of her dark skin and hair. She had just a few men with her, but she pledged to defend the castle. When the English, led by the Lord of Salisbury, requested that she surrender, she sent him a bold reply that she would keep her house. After he had hurled boulders from catapults into the castle walls, Agnes sent oot her maids onto the ramparts with handkerchiefs to wipe the debris from the walls and sing ditties as they worked."

Caught up in the tale, Elysande smiled and moved closer.

"Angered by her boldness," he continued, feeding his audience more. "Salisbury rolled oot a huge batterin' ram with a wooden roof to protect the men underneath. They pounded the doors, once, twice. The doors cracked and the people inside fled, terrified fer their lives. But Agnes was unmoved and ready fer such an attack. She ordered large boulders—ones that the English catapults provided—to be dropped down from the ramparts. They crashed into the wooden roof and killed many of the men beneath. The rest fled every which way."

Some of his audience laughed and shook their heads in awe of Agnes Randolf's cleverness.

"Winter passed and spring arrived," he continued. "Salisbury knew that Dunbar's winter food supply had to be gravely low. And 'twas. Agnes and her men wouldna have lasted another month. I know because 'tis when I arrived with Lord Alexander Ramsay of Dalhousie with supplies. We entered the castle in two boats through a half-submerged tunnel below the castle.

"True to Agnes' nature, she had fresh bread and wine sent out to Lord Salisbury, lettin' him know they were strong and well fed."

People around Elysande clapped. Indeed, she clapped, as well, loving the heroics of this woman, a woman like her mother.

"But the best of all," the stranger told them with a furtive smile, "was when, in desperation, Salisbury had Agnes' brother, the Earl of Moray, brought forth and threatened to kill him if she didna surrender. But Agnes pointed out that should her brother be killed, childless as he was, she would inherit the title and become the next earl. Finally,

Salisbury retreated, knowin' he couldna beat her. His men sang a ballad to her as they marched away.

> 'She makes a stir in tower and trench,
> That brawlin', boisterous, Scottish wench;
> Came I early, came I late.
> I found Agnes at the gate.'"

Everyone who had gathered around him clapped and cheered when his story came to an end.

As the small crowd began to disperse, his gaze met hers and he moved toward her. She waited for him to say something. When he finally tried—tearing his eyes off the thin laurel wreath around her brow—he stumbled over the few words he managed. "I...ye...ehm." She blushed at how he looked about to fall at her feet.

Taking notice of the MacPhersons' enraptured guest, her uncle, Torin, ventured over with laughter dancing across his wide, green eyes. He wore his gold-splashed hair plaited and pulled back at his temples, but gossamer curls still managed to escape and fall softly around his eyes.

"Raphael, son of Robert Cameron," he introduced, "my niece, Elysande, daughter of Cain MacPherson."

At his introduction, Raphael and Elysande's smiles faded. Their fathers were enemies. They might as well turn around and leave now. Nothing could ever come of them.

Elysande had the urge to pout, but she was no child. And why should she? Just because the woman Raphael Cameron admired most was strong and intelligent? Because his stunning green eyes were compelling and curious about her? Because she wanted to brush his hair off his cheek...and run her fingertips over his full, curved lips? Because she would never see him again after Hogmanay? There were a dozen more reasons for her sudden sadness.

Her father would never—"Elysande!" His voice thundered

through the hall. He didn't wait for her response, but stormed toward her. "Go find yer mother."

"Cain, they are just meetin'," her uncle risked.

"Just meetin'?" Cainnech MacPherson's eyes hardened with dark intent. Her uncle took a step back. "First ye invite them to the stronghold, and now ye are handin' them my only daughter!"

Just a moment now! No one was handing her over to anyone, but Elysande knew that arguing with her father now was pointless.

"Mr. MacPherson," the foolish, seemingly fearless Raphael Cameron said. "I would never dishonor yer daughter. I am here fer peace, not a bride."

"That is good to hear," her father growled.

Elysande wished she felt the same relief at the declaration.

"Otherwise," her father promised, leaning in and aiming his most lethal glare at Robbie Cameron's son. "I would skin ye alive and then hang ye by yer ankles, naked and skinless in the cold until ye died."

Elysande closed her eyes. She didn't expect to see Raphael still standing there when she opened them again. None of the men who tried to court her had stood up to her father.

But Raphael hadn't run. He was still there.

Chapter Two

Raphael would have a serious talk with Torin MacPherson later about dishonesty. Torin had vowed that his two brothers wanted peace as he did. On that vow, Raphael had begged his father to accept the MacPhersons' invitation to their Christmastide celebration and staying for Hogmanay. Not long after they arrived, Raphael had discovered that the most merciless brother of the three, Cain, did not want peace. Not surprisingly, he also felt very strongly about a Cameron anywhere near his bonny daughter.

Elysande.

In all his travels, Raphael had never met anyone so exquisite, so utterly perfect to his eyes. When he'd first found her among the many faces of his audience, he'd wanted to say something, but he couldn't. He'd never lost his power of speech before—or had it been his inability to form a coherent thought that stopped him from speaking? Why did she have to be MacPherson's daughter? How was he ever expected to forget her luminously big, blue eyes that spoke their own language, or her mouth…hell, her mouth was the shape of an expertly carved bow, pink and plump and parted with bated breath, waiting for him to say something!

"Father," she spoke, denying her father's request to go find her mother. He didn't seem to mind.

She spoke and Raphael fell like one enchanted by the sound of her, by the sight of her long, loose curls draping her shoulder and secured by her laurel circlet. She looked like a forest angel, otherworldly and mesmerizing. "Mr. Cameron was just tellin' the story of Lady Agnes Randolf of Dunbar Castle."

"Hmm," her father growled, still eyeing him. "I know of her."

"She reminds me of mother," beautiful Elysande told him. Then she turned to Raphael and rattled his world around in her hands with her smile. He had spoken the truth. He hadn't come here for a bride, but now that he'd seen Elysande MacPherson, he wondered if there was a man in the stronghold who had already captured her heart.

He glanced at her glaring father and doubted it.

"My mother defended her castle in England with the same tenacity as Lady Agnes."

"Yer mother is English?" Raphael asked with a raised brow aimed at her father. This was a surprise that the fearsome Highland warrior had married his enemy.

"Norman," her father corrected on a warning growl.

"She knew my father's troops were comin'," Elysande continued, drawing Raphael's attention to her...along with her father's. "So with the help of her loyal villagers, they turned the surroundin' forest into a battlefield. They constructed walkways in the trees and built traps that could be set off from above."

"We lost nine men at her hands," said another Highlander who had just joined them. He had a long scar running down his face, and a wee girl in his arms. "She didna give up even after we took the castle. Remember, Cain? She poisoned Nicky."

"Aye," her father nodded, his scowl, finally fading into something warm. "She escaped the dungeon and tried to kill me in my own bed."

The men laughed with admiration for her. Raphael was surprised and gladdened that such warriors felt as they did.

When the woman they were speaking of entered the hall, Elysande called to her. "Mother! Come join us!"

Aleysia d'Argentan MacPherson approached with her arm hooked onto the elbow of an older priest. She was even lovelier than Raphael expected by the looks of her daughter. Her skin was as white as winter. Her eyes were as green as trees in summer. Her long, plaited hair was dark with a broad streak of gray shot through above her right temple.

After her arrival, more people came to share memories of a castle called Lismoor and the surrender of the Scot's fiercest warrior.

Raphael enjoyed the stories and, more, the fact that Cain MacPherson finally forgot about him.

He caught Elysande's eyes and she motioned for him to meet her at a long, nearby table. He did as she silently requested, doubting the good of his decision…of his mind and followed her. He looked toward the table where his father was sitting and drinking wassail with the youngest MacPherson brother, Nicholas.

"Dinna worry," Elysande reassured him. "If anyone can win him over, 'tis Uncle Nicky."

"Ye dinna know my father," Raphael said, shaking his head. "Robbie Cameron is a cantankerous man, always sour and ready to fight. I worry I made the wrong decision in comin' here and in trustin' yer uncle, Torin, when he had proposed the idea of comin' together fer Christmastide. Let our friendships grow and animosity end and let there be peace. It felt good talkin' aboot it."

Raphael wanted nothing more. He was determined to strive for it. He'd been so since his mother lost her life to a band of Privers, also rivals of the Camerons. The Privers were nearly wiped out in his father's rage. He and his small army of men, including Raphael, had killed two hundred men, leaving their wives as widows and their children as orphans.

Raphael wanted to avoid battle again. He would do almost anything, including dine and drink with the enemy and try to make them enemies no more. But he hadn't bargained on meeting the most beautiful woman in Scotland, or that he would like sitting with her, talking to her, looking at her.

"How do ye feel aboot peace, Elysande?" He bowed his head, hoping he hadn't been too forward all this time using her Christian name. "May I call ye Elysande? I like the sound of it."

She nodded then rested her elbow on the table and her chin inside her hand. "I like how it sounds when ye say it. And I shall call ye Raphael. Ye do know that Raphael is the name of an angel, aye?"

He laughed softly. "I dinna take after my namesake."

"How d'ye know that?" she asked. He thought that if she wanted him to be an angel, he would give up everything that displeased God—what was he saying? He was a fool. His father would never...*her* father would never...

He should get up, leave her company. He could go sit with his father and learn a little about Nicholas MacPherson. But he didn't want to leave her.

"Aboot peace..."

He blinked. "Aye?"

She lifted her chin out of her hand and crossed her arms on the table. "I am not sure I stand on yer and Uncle Torin's side."

"Och, dear lady, ye twist the knife." He pretended to be holding on to said knife at his heart and writhed in pain.

"Fergive me, dear sir, but with Robert the Bruce dead and his young son on the throne, we dinna have the guarantee of safety we once enjoyed with his father. If we begin lettin' everyone into the stronghold, 'twill no longer be a stronghold. Still..."

"Still?" he asked, praying there was hope for her.

"If ye become the next chief, I would trust ye to keep yer word."

"And ye would give peace a chance between our clans?"

"Aye," she promised with a smile that softened her large eyes. "But 'twill take a miracle to change my father's mind."

"Ah, well, then 'tis a good thing I know people," he said, glancing up—referring to his angelic name.

They laughed together until a shadow covered her. Raphael looked up to see a tall fellow with yellow hair and dark eyes staring down at her.

"Ellie, I was lookin' fer ye. I wasna expectin' to find ye sittin' alone with a stranger."

Unrattled, she glanced up and narrowed her eyes on him. "Where were ye expectin' to find me, Hugh?" She raised her brows and waited for him to answer.

"With yer kin," he answered. Then he looked over his shoulder at the first generation of MacPhersons and their friends now sitting together at another table, all engaged in drinking and laughing.

Raphael's father was at the table as well, sitting near Nicholas. He was drinking but not laughing.

"But I see Cain is distracted. Shall I bring the matter up with him?"

Raphael saw Elysande's anger boil to the surface, her eyes becoming the same icy color as her father's.

"Raphael Cameron," Raphael introduced himself. His voice achieved what he wanted. The man's attention shifted instantly to him. Raphael offered him a friendly smile.

"Hugh Tanner."

"Mr. Tanner, fergive me fer sittin' with yer wife." He began to rise from his chair.

"I am not his wife." Elysande's voice stopped him.

Raphael knew it already because if she was anyone's wife, someone would have mentioned it by now. Still, he stopped rising and glanced at Elysande. "Betrothed?"

"No," she told him, soothing his racing heart. "And I am beginnin' to hope I never am."

Raphael smiled, liking her boldness, and sat back down. "In that case, Mr. Tanner, ye are free to join us, but I will remain where I am."

Hugh Tanner had other ideas. He reached down and grasped Raphael by the collar and pulled him to his feet.

Raphael was here for peace.

It took an instant to remind himself before he reacted, and an instant for a younger version of Nicholas MacPherson to reach them and yank him free.

"Hugh, that will be enough!" the younger MacPherson said in a hushed voice and through clenched teeth. "The Camerons are our guests." He turned Tanner around and gave his back a shove. "Now go sit somewhere else before you start a damned war."

"Elias MacPherson," the brawny Highlander greeted and dragged a chair from its place. "Call me Eli."

Raphael introduced himself and gave Elias a more thorough looking over. "Ye were on Lord Ramsay's ship when we came to Dunbar last spring."

Elias' face broke into a smile. "Aye. I heard your tale earlier. You were on the ship, too."

They toasted a drink to Black Agnes and reminisced for a bit. Then, Raphael looked over Elias' shoulder at Hugh and shook his head. "I wish there to be peace and havin' him hate me willna do. I wonder if ye would ask him to come back."

Elias stared at him for a moment—mayhap two, as if he'd just sprouted another nose. Then he pushed out of his chair, pounded his way to where Hugh was sitting, dragged him up by the back of his plaid, and returned with him to the table. He ripped a chair from under the table and sat Tanner in it.

"There," he said to Raphael. "Is that better?"

Raphael smiled at him and nodded then continued to smile for the next three hours while he shared food and drinks with Elysande and the rest of her siblings and cousins.

When the end of the night finally came, Raphael hated bidding Elysande good eve. He could have stayed awake for another twenty hours talking to her. But it was best to let her go.

That was what he told himself until he fell asleep and dreamed of her.

Chapter Three

Elysande dressed herself in a semi-sheer chemise and soft, white, woolen hose to her knees. She donned her purple kirtle, the one her dear friend, Margaret, embroidered with delicate swirls of gold thread along the hem of its full skirts and long, fitted sleeves that covered her knuckles. She wore a crimson cotehardie, fitted at the waist and flaring outward with a purple linen lining. She plaited her thick, dark hair into a braid that hung over her shoulder and secured a thin crimson veil to her head.

Someone knocked at the door to her room in her parents' manor house.

The door opened and without invitation, though her dear cousins needed none, her cousin, Adela, entered the room and threw herself onto Elysande's bed.

"Happy Christmas morn, El! Oh!" she exclaimed, sitting up and taking notice of her cousin. "You look breathtaking!" Before Elysande could thank her, she closed her eyes and took in a great breath. "Do you smell the cakes and shortbread baking? 'Tis heavenly!"

Adela was ten and six and full of enthusiasm for just about anything. She was also the bonniest lass alive in Elysande's estimation. She resembled her mother, Aunt Julianna, Uncle Nicky's wife, with flowing red hair and large, dark eyes, and a wide smile. Though separated by three years, they were very close. Elysande's cousins of her own age were males. She loved them all, but she and Adela always stuck together, wrong or right, through everything.

"Stand and let me take a look at ye," Elysande said. Her tender smile widened when her cousin did as she asked. "I love how the green of yer dress brings out the red of yer hair. Ye will still every heart."

Her cousin laughed, but Elysande believed it. There were many offers for her hand, but Uncle Nicky refused them all. He wasn't as bad as Elysande's father. He did allow one suitor to court her for a little while before sending him away. He told the young man that if he truly loved his daughter, he would return in two years.

"Tell me about Mr. Cameron," Adela suggested furtively and patted the bed beside her. "Elias was discussing him with my father when I awoke. Elias told him about Mr. Cameron and Hugh. Father said he believes Mr. Cameron truly wants peace."

Elysande agreed with her cousin. "He is peculiar, Adela," she told her. "He didna shrink from my father when he was threatened. He did not run away, no, he went off with me to a nearby table, where we would be alone."

Elysande put her fingers under Adela's chin and closed her mouth. "I know," she laughed. "I like him, Adela. What shall I do? My father—"

"I know," her cousin consoled. "But my father says that Uncle Torin likes him, too. Mayhap they can convince Uncle Cain to change his mind. Brother Simon says that anything is possible with God, aye? And 'tis Christmas Day!"

"And he is named after the archangel Raphael!" Elysande added.

They both gasped, and then collapsed on the bed with laughter.

"Get up. We will wrinkle our dresses," Elysande said, sobering. She turned to her cousin, sitting up and slinging her legs over the side. "What shall I do in the meantime?"

Adela's deep, sable eyes gleamed from within. "Have a merry time."

ELYSANDE STOOD WITHIN the loving wings of her parents and eldest brother, Tristan, to her right and her three other brothers to her left. All their eyes were set on Father Timothy at the altar of their church reciting from the Gospel of John. The scent of melting tallow wax assailed her senses and made her smile. It was a familiar scent that she loved.

The church was heavily decorated in mountain laurel and holly and though cold seeped through the walls, candles burned everywhere—dozens being added for Christmas—and gave the church a warm and inviting atmosphere.

The rest of her kin filled the church, singing, praying, and hungry to eat of the wonderful dishes to be served in the great hall.

A few benches behind her stood Raphael and his father, along with their men. Could she feel his eyes on her, or was it just her hopeful heart? She ached to turn around and look at him. Once, she did. For just an instant, she turned and caught sight of him. He was looking at her and smiled. She returned the gesture and turned away before anyone noticed. But Uncle Torin saw her and seemed quite pleased. She remembered him last eve, looking just as happy when *he* introduced them. What was he up to, she wondered? Raphael had mentioned regretting trusting her uncle. What had Torin promised him?

Suddenly, her heart wrenched within her. Had her uncle promised *her*? She turned, boldly this time, and glared at Raphael. Was he doing all this for peace, or to have her? She moved her angry stare to her uncle. How dare he connive to give her away as if she were a prized horse?

Tears stung her eyes and she turned away and bit her tongue. She wanted to ask him if she was correct. Should she tell her father? No! There was no need to start a war. She would speak to her uncle after mass. She wasn't sure she was even thinking clearly. Uncle Torin loved her. The father of all boys, he'd always treated her like a beloved daughter. Of course he wouldn't trade her for peace! He didn't truly even care about peace. He invited the Camerons to the stronghold and sought peace as a gift for his wife. Aunt Braya was the one who wanted peace. Before she married Uncle Torin, she'd been a border reiver, fighting other clans for food. It was hard for Elysande to imagine her aunt brandishing a sword, for Braya was as slight as a veil, with pale blonde hair and wide, genuine smiles. But Elysande had seen her practicing and she was deadlier than some of the men. *She* wanted the feud to end. Peacefully.

Would her uncle have made the alliance with a promise of marriage?

Elysande didn't think she'd mind being married to Raphael, but it would be her decision, not her uncle's. Was peace the reason Raphael had spent the night celebrating at her table? She had to know the truth.

When the mass ended, she excused herself from her parents and brothers, with the excuse of wanting to ask Uncle Torin to recite one of his poems later.

Her father playfully begged her not to ask. That is, she thought he was being playful. She wasn't sure he had forgiven his brother for inviting their enemies for Christmastide.

"Now, Father, ye know ye love his odes, and him along with them," she teased and broke away from him. The instant he could no longer see her face, her smile faded and she set her hard gaze on her uncle.

"Elysande."

She stopped at the sound of Raphael's voice and turned slowly to look at him.

Oh, she shouldn't have. She couldn't think straight with him so close. He looked especially handsome this morn dressed in a black doublet and hose with his blue and black plaid draped over his shoulder and around his waist. His black hair was loose and straight, and fell like sensual fingers to the tops of his shoulders, caressing his neck.

"I was hopin' ye would allow me to sit with ye again while we eat and celebrate the birth of our Lord." He smiled, not really giving her a chance to decline him emphatically the way she should.

"I…" She looked at her uncle about to head for the doors. She was tempted to look over her shoulder at her father to know if he was looking her way. She had never deceived him, and she wouldn't start now. "I would like that," she told him with a soft smile. "But first, join me while I speak a moment to my uncle."

He agreed, and they walked together toward the doors. If he thought to share a word with her while they went, he'd have to pick up his pace.

"Uncle Torin," Elysande called as she hurried to him. After a quick kiss to her dearest Aunt Braya and her cousins, she pulled Raphael forward.

"Ye already know Raphael Cameron."

Her uncle offered Raphael a bright smile and pulled him closer for a heftier pat on the back. "Aye, how d'ye like it here so far, lad?"

Elysande tried to keep her mouth shut but she could not. "Enough to wed me, no doubt!"

Everyone standing around her opened their eyes wide. Her aunt, who was no exception, shooed her sons away then turned back to her. "Elysande, are ye ill?" She stared into Elysande's eyes as if trying to silently convey the need to close up her niece's mouth.

"What was that I just heard ye say aboot weddin' someone, Elysande?" her father asked, coming close.

"Elysande was recitin' a line from one of my poems," Uncle Torin told him.

"Oh?" her father asked, eyeing Raphael suspiciously. "Which one?"

"The one aboot Alisdair MacLauchlan's long snout," her uncle answered. "Would ye like to hear some of it?

"There was a young fool—"

Her father held up his palm. "No more." He took a step toward the doorway with the rest of his family then turned back to Raphael. "Ye, come with me."

No. Elysande tried to stop it. If her father got Raphael alone, he would frighten him away. "Father—"

"Of course," Raphael cut her off. "I was hopin' fer a moment or two with ye, Commander."

Elysande watched them leave. Out of her sight. What if her father killed him? *Dinna be ridiculous, Elysande,* she told herself. *He would never go so far.*

"El, what was that ootburst aboot?" her uncle asked, pulling her thoughts away from Raphael running away.

"I know all aboot yer plan to have us marry fer peace. Ye will never convince Father and ye will never convince me."

"What the bloody hell are ye talkin' aboot, gel?" he exclaimed. "Braya, check her fer fever."

Her aunt came closer and reached out but Elysande moved out of the way. "I'm well, I assure ye. Ye traded me fer peace, Uncle Torin." She hated herself for it, but tears stung her eyes.

He gathered her in his arms immediately and kissed the top of her head. "My wee gel. I love ye as my own. Ye are the daughter we never had. Aye, Braya, my love?"

"Aye," her aunt agreed, closing her arms around them both.

"I'm hurt that ye would think such a thing of me," he said, crushing her heart. "But now that ye mention it, if ye werena opposed to such a union, I would be on yer side."

She almost smiled. But she remembered her outburst and nearly fainted. She never wanted to face Raphael again. She would rather be swallowed up by the ground and never return.

Chapter Four

Raphael stood with Cain MacPherson in the great hall sipping *athole brose*, a drink made from oats, honey, and whisky. The honey was sweet and the whisky was potent. His father sat at the MacPhersons' table again, sharing a word with Cain's wife and another beautiful woman with flaming red locks who, judging from where she sat during mass, was Nicholas' wife.

"Cameron," Cain addressed him menacingly. "I dinna know why ye are here. I only know yer kin are deceitful, dishonorable men and have been fer centuries."

"The Camerons say the same aboot ye, Commander," Raphael countered. Of course he feared the commander. But that didn't mean he would recoil in fear. "Ye are infamous fer fightin' mercilessly at Bannockburn. Yer brother, Torin, is known fer his great ability to deceive and bring down strongholds from within. Less is known of the youngest, Nicholas—"

"Leave him oot of this," Cain warned.

Raphael nodded. "Verra well. I am not my kin, nor am I my father. I dinna agree with his ideas aboot peace. I believe the feuds could and should end. Enough blood has been shed."

Cain narrowed his eyes on him. "Those are nice words, but unless yer father is gone, there will be no peace between us. And just in case there are other thoughts swirlin' aboot in yer head, stay fer another moment. There is somethin' I want ye to hear."

He put his hand on Raphael's shoulder and called attention. Everyone looked up and set their gazes on him and Raphael. "Today is a day filled with blessings, the first of which I give to my daughter."

Raphael's heartbeat sped up.

"Today, I announce Elysande's betrothal to Hugh Tanner."

Some people cheered. Elysande stood up, looking pale and ill and ran from the hall. Raphael pulled his shoulder from beneath her father's hand. He was angry. He would not back down.

"Ye would hurt her to prove a point to me? I didna think ye a fool, Commander."

"Watch yer tongue, Cameron," Cain warned through a tight jaw.

Now was the time to still his tongue, but he couldn't. He understood her father hated him. But to wed her to Hugh Tanner to keep them apart? 'Twas cruel to her and he wanted her father to know. "He is belittlin' and arrogant *toward yer daughter,* usin' her love, respect, fear, or whatever she feels toward ye to threaten her," he said. "I didna pummel his face beneath the heel of my boot last eve because I came here fer peace. Ye made a terrible mistake, Commander. Her husband will own her, not love her. That is what ye sentenced her to."

He turned without waiting for a response and left the hall.

ELYSANDE LEFT THE fortress and drew her fur-lined cloak closer around her neck. A thin layer of frost covered the hundreds of acres of wilderness and hills where the MacPhersons' cattle and sheep grazed. The air was brisk and turned her breath white.

She didn't care how cold it was. She had to get away from her father, her uncle, and Raphael. They all thought to *think* for her! She didn't want to believe her uncle was innocent because then she would have to admit that she blurted out that Raphael liked it there *enough to wed her, no doubt!* Oh, she thought she could hear her bones rattling with mortification. She had to get away.

And her father! Her tears whipped off her cheeks on a bracing gust of wind. How could he announce her betrothal to Hugh when he hadn't even told her? Had he planned it or was his action a result of trying to keep her from Raphael? She let out a short scream that was carried away on the wind.

This was what she needed. To scream a little without being heard by a fortress full of people. She kept going, walking farther away, trying to think clearly about what to do. Would she have to marry Hugh? She changed her mind. She didn't want to marry him anymore! Mayhap if she just told her father how she felt...no. He wouldn't listen. His caution toward his enemies was too strong.

The wind was growing stronger, snapping her cloak and skirts around her ankles. Puffs of white swirled around her feet as the howling wind swept up the frost. She looked up toward the hills and tried to see if any of the shepherds had come out and tended to their sheep and cattle. But she couldn't see that far. In fact, the drifting, swirling snow had grown stronger, pulling at her hood, burning her face with the icy cold. She should have known better than to venture so far with the unpredictable weather of the Highlands.

She turned around, cursing at the weather for not letting her go off by herself. She had to get back inside. Frustrated, she shouted as loud as she could just one more time before she realized she couldn't see the stronghold.

Dear God, help, she thought as panic settled over her. She just had to keep walking straight. She couldn't open her eyes. They stung and watered. Even if she could open them, all she would see was white.

White. Everywhere.

CHAPTER FIVE

Raphael left the hall and, in his search for Elysande, was informed by a man carrying a shepherd's crook that he had seen her outside.

Collecting his cloak, Raphael left and ran into the bracing cold, toward the stable. None of the stalls were empty. She was on foot. She wouldn't have gone far. The wind was increasing steadily and filled with icy mist. Another five breaths and more snow began to fall.

"Elysande!" he shouted. Where would she have gone? The howling wind answered him. She wouldn't be able to hear him. What should he do? Go back for his horse? Run back to the hall and get her father?

He ran while he could still see the structure and burst into the great hall. He didn't look at anyone in particular. He had to hurry. He had to get out there and find her.

"Elysande!" he shouted. Every eye turned to him. "She is outside! There is a storm—I must find her!"

People were moving, running, but he was already gone.

He rushed outside and was able to see the heavy gates moving back and forth in the wind, unbolted, unguarded. The shepherd he saw inside had just gone beyond the wall, hadn't he? Did he leave the gates open?

An instant later and the gates disappeared–along with everything else as snow filled the air and blinded the eyes.

Raphael ran toward the sound of the gates creaking open and closed. He rushed past them and out into the wilderness.

"Elysande!" he shouted as loud as he could. He was sure his heart had almost left his body through his mouth. He knew she wouldn't hear him. Which way would she go? Toward the forest to be alone? Or toward the hills? To a shepherd's home, mayhap? He tried to look around. Which way were the trees, the hills? He remembered where they were yesterday when he and his father had arrived, so he turned the opposite way now and ran left, toward the forest.

After what her father had done, she would want to be alone, not knocking on doors. She might have tried to turn toward the hills, but she hadn't had time for a detour.

"Elysande!" he shouted, despite the wind.

He tripped and fell over something soft. A body! Elysande!

With his heart racing like the wind, he sat up and gathered her in his arms. She did not respond. With tears stinging his eyes, he pressed his ear to her chest and listened for a heartbeat.

He heard one! Oh, he gave thanks. She was alive! He had to keep her that way until he got her back to the hall or to a shelter.

He cradled her in his arms and stood up with her. How was he going to do this, he thought while he tied his cloak around them with the fingers of one hand?

Holding her close, he tried to let his body's heat fill her. He breathed on her neck, her cheek. He tucked her hands close and shivered from her cold.

"Come with me," he heard a male voice say in front of him.

Raphael had no other option. He put Elysande over his shoulder so that his hands were free, and placed one of them on the man's shoulder, letting him lead.

They walked through the curtain on a path that was seemingly easy for this man to follow thanks to a barking dog leading him. A short while later, they came to a cottage with candlelit windows and warmth inside.

Warmth.

Raphael set Elysande on the bed of Adam of Aberdeen, one of seven shepherds for the MacPhersons. After much thanks, he added more wood to the fire and sat on the edge of the bed while Adam saw to her.

"All will be well, but ye must undress her. Just to her chemise," the shepherd told him when Raphael began to refuse. "Her clothes are wet and freezin'. Ye must also remove yer shirt and get into bed with her. Give her yer heat. I myself would do it, but I know her father and I want to keep my head."

Raphael stared at him for a moment and wondered if the shepherd was jesting. He decided he wasn't and cast Elysande a worried look. He couldn't let her die.

He undressed her with shaking fingers, not because of fear of her father, but because he didn't want her to awaken and think he was trying to have his way with her in her sickly condition. And because he wished he were undressing her with her consenting, eager eyes on him. He peeled off her clothes and when he saw that her chemise was sheer, he pulled the bed covers over her to keep her feminine shape away from the shepherd's—and his own—eyes.

He pulled off his cloak and his plaid, doublet and shirt. Everything fell to the floor until his upper body was bare. He pulled away the covering and climbed into bed beside her. He closed his eyes. Her father would kill him. How close was the commander to them? He asked the shepherd, but the shepherd didn't know.

With nothing more to do for now, Raphael held her, covering her entire body as the shepherd directed. Her body was warming up and he did all he could not to become too aware of her soft curves and firm peaks against him.

"We should notify her father," he told Adam the shepherd to help keep his mind off things.

"D'ye want to go oot there?" the shepherd asked. "I dinna. 'Twill have to wait until the storm passes."

Raphael didn't want to go out. He certainly didn't want to leave the bed, but her kin would be sick with worry. No, he wanted to hold her and make certain she was well. He wanted to breathe the faint scent of mountain laurel in her hair, left there by the drooping wreath stuck in her veil.

He pulled it free with gentle, slightly less trembling fingers. He removed her veil and stared at her face like one caught in the beauty of a summer sunrise after a long, dark winter.

"I'll make some tea," said the shepherd and left the small room.

Raphael took in the slight slope of her nose, the delectable bow shape of her mouth, the alluring curves of her cheek and jaw. He wanted to kiss her. He ran his palms down her back and then closed his eyes and said a silent prayer to stay strong. She needed his heat. He could hold her without losing his mind…or his heart.

"Elysande, please awaken, lass. I need to find yer father."

She opened her eyes with a flutter of dark, lush lashes. For one blissful moment, she smiled into his eyes. He knew in that moment that he wanted to wake up next to her every morning for the rest of his life. Then her smile faded.

"Why d'ye need to find him? What…?" She suddenly realized where she was. In his arms, against his bare chest. "What are ye doin'?" She tried to wiggle away from him. He released her, but she fell back when she tried to rise up from the bed.

"Elysande," he said in a soft voice, "ye were almost dead in the snow, barely breathin', lass. There is a storm—" He reached for her when she made her second attempt to leave the bed.

"Raphael." She leaned back in the bed, too weary to get up. "Go find my father. Dinna stay here another instant." She spoke the words and yet she suddenly clutched at him as if she didn't want him to go.

"If he finds ye here alone and undressed with me, he will kill ye."

Raphael nodded. "I am goin'. But I hate to leave ye."

Her smile softened on him, making his heart palpitate. "How did ye find me, Raphael?"

"I fell over ye." He laughed at himself, knowing it was the least heroic thing he could say.

She lifted her pale, delicate hand to her mouth and laughed with him. Raphael understood in that moment why her father was so protective of her. Losing her, seeing her hurt in this violent world would drive Raphael mad. He understood.

He wanted to return to her and wrap her in his arms again. He wanted to feel her heartbeat as close as his own. But he had to find her father and let him know that his daughter was alive.

He left her and went to the next room to look for the shepherd who hadn't returned with the tea. He found Adam in the kitchen still preparing it.

When he heard what Raphael meant to do, Adam gave him more clothes to wear and two extra cloaks beneath his fur one.

Raphael thanked him and returned to bid Elysande farewell. He didn't want to leave her. He didn't know if he'd ever see her again. Her father was out there, ready, Raphael was sure, to die finding her. Would things be better for him and Elysande if her father was dead? He could stay here with her and let Cain MacPherson possibly die in the storm.

No. Whatever the outcome, Raphael would find him and give him back his daughter.

He went to her and knelt beside the bed, taking her hand in his. "I want ye to know, Elysande MacPherson, that I love ye. I dinna care if I just met ye, lass. Ye have taken hold of my heart, making it ready to risk everythin', even my own life fer ye. I love ye. Whatever happens, I want ye to know that."

He gently swiped a tear from her eye and then held his finger to her mouth. He didn't want to know her reply. If he died, he wanted to believe she loved him. If she didn't, he didn't want to know. He stood up and quietly left the cottage.

And stepped into the howling, white wind.

Chapter Six

Cain pulled his fur-lined cloak closer around his face, leaving only a narrow slit between his cloak and his hood. He could barely see two feet in front of him. But he knew his way. Even if he didn't, he would travel the pathway to Hades to find her. His and Aleysia's only daughter. Their treasure, cherished beyond measure. If anything terrible were to befall her…he couldn't finish the thought.

He was freezing. Even wrapped in wool and fox, the wind found a way to get through to his bones. But the colder he became the more his determination to find her grew. He prayed that she'd found shelter, or her way back to the fortress. He prayed because if she was out here lost, she was already dead. Tears stung his eyes.

Please God, no. Please send help on this Christmas night.

This was all his fault. If he hadn't announced her betrothal to Hugh Tanner, she never would have run away. Was Raphael Cameron correct about Hugh? Was he using her love, respect, fear, or whatever she felt toward him to threaten her? He'd tried to find out by pulling Tanner aside and questioning him. Tanner profusely denied the charges.

Either way, if Cain had her back, he would listen to her. If she didn't want to marry Hugh Tanner, then she wouldn't marry him. But what if she wanted to marry—

He hit into something soft, yet inflexible.

"Who is there?"

Cain scowled hearing Robbie Cameron's voice. What the hell was he doing out here. Cain asked him.

"My son apparently followed yer reckless daughter into the storm in an attempt to save her. Now, he may be dead because of her."

Cain didn't know how to answer that accusation. Young Cameron went out into the freezing, blinding storm after her. Hugh Tanner did not, nor did he even show concern over her when Cain was questioning him. "I will find them," Cain muttered and pushed past him. He hated that he'd just promised to save Cameron's son, but it was the man's—even if it was his enemy—bairn.

"I'm comin' with ye," Cameron said, placing his hand on Cain's shoulder.

"No."

"MacPherson," Cameron shouted over the wind, "d'ye want to fight aboot it here and now while our bairns could be fightin' fer their lives?"

Cain huffed and then moved onward with his enemy Robbie Cameron holding on.

They pushed their way through the wind and snow and then Cameron stopped and grabbed hold of Cain's arm. "I heard somethin'!" He spun around, ignoring Cain hitting his hand away.

"Dinna twist me around, Cameron! If I lose my sense of…" he let his words trail off. Which way was he facing? How many times did Cameron pull him around? His stomach sank. He felt like killing his unwanted companion. He listened for any sounds and when he heard nothing, he swore an oath and punched at the air, hoping to hit Cameron, whom he could no longer see at all.

"I dinna know which way to go now, ye fool!"

"But I thought I heard somethin'," Robbie defended.

"Ye heard the wind!" Cain shouted at him. "And now we will most likely die here." He moved away from Cameron and turned to the left. The path toward the shepherds' homes was this way he believed. But who knew for certain?

"I think we turned right," said Cameron, passing him. "Whichever way ye were headin' should be—"

"Cameron?" Cain called out after a few moments passed without another word from him. "Cameron, what the hell—!"

"MacPherson, dinna take another step!" Cameron screamed out from below him. "'Tis a cliff! I fell. I...I am holdin' on to somethin'...a branch. One foot is on a perch, the other is hangin' down. I dinna know how far. I need yer help."

Now Cain knew where they were. He remained still. It was more of a drop-off than a cliff, but it was high enough above the river Garry to die from the fall.

Here it was. A way to get rid of his enemy once and for all. Every summer, who was it that tried to steal his cattle? The Camerons. Who laid traps for his kin when they were on the road so that they could do nothing but watch while their horses and any goods they had were taken from them? The Camerons. Who killed his good friend and second in command, Amish? Robbie Cameron.

But it was Christmas. And Cameron was his guest, thanks to his idiot brother.

He grumbled under his breath and knelt down on all fours.

"MacPherson." His voice rose to Cain's ears. "I wanted ye to know this, but I was too much of a coward to tell ye to yer face, but in all our raids and skirmishes, I never meant to kill Amish. I respected him as a warrior too much to kill him. We were fightin' and I swung left thinkin' that was the way he was goin', but he turned at the last moment to take a swipe at me and my blade fell on him and caused his death. I was sorry fer it. I still am."

Cain looked down, letting his vision settle on the dark mass below.

"Will ye aid me, MacPherson?"

"Aye," Cain grumbled louder, wondering how he would. There was no rope around and no vines to help. His cloaks and wrappings would have to do. He quickly tore them off then began tying them together to form a rope.

"It willna hold!" Cameron called up when Cain told him what he was doing.

"'Twill hold," Cain called back confidently. "Ye dinna know the sewin' skills of Berengaria and Margaret." He smiled into the white, thinking of Nicky's mother and dearest friend.

"Tie it around yer waist or wrap it many times around yer wrist. Call to me when ye are ready to come up."

He prayed it would work while he dug in his heels and braced his weight in the snow. No one in the stronghold would believe he didn't kill his enemy when he had the chance.

"Ready!" Cameron called.

"God, help us." Cain tested the weight for a moment and wrapped both his wrists in the fabric and began to pull. He was about twenty breaths in when his muscles began to stiffen and cramp. Still he pulled, grinding his teeth, praying for more time. Just a little more time.

"I think a knot just came undone!" Cameron shouted. He was closer.

No! Do not let him fall this close to safety!

Suddenly, the weight was lifted and the makeshift rope went slack. Cain's belly sank. Even though Cameron's apology was given in order to save his life, Cain believed it and thought it was good to hear.

He heard another male voice, and then Cameron's! The white fog was dissipating. He watched a hooded figure bent over and pulling Cameron up the rest of the way.

"How did ye find us, Son?"

Cameron's son, Raphael.

"I followed yer voice."

The one who came out in search of Elysande!

"My daughter!" Cain said from the ground, taking a moment or two to gather his breath and calm his muscles. "Did ye find her?"

"Yer daughter is fine and in good care thanks to Adam, one of yer shepherds. She is restin' and anxiously awaits word of ye."

"Restin' from what?" Cain asked, straightening on his feet.

"I found her lyin' in the snowdrifts. She was close to death."

Cain gasped and stepped back. "Take me to her!"

The young Cameron agreed but checked to make sure his father could make the journey.

"Today, ye were given a gift of findin' folks in a storm," Cain gave in on the way up the hill and said something Father Timothy would approve of. "Ye arrived just in time to save my daughter and yer father. God is good."

"Aye, He is," Raphael replied. "I am verra thankful to have found them both. They are important—"

Cain's expression suddenly grew dark. "Who is Adam? I dinna have a shepherd by that name."

Neither one remarked but turned to the silhouette of different sized cottages on the hill and then they ran.

CHAPTER SEVEN

ELYSANDE STOOD AT the entrance to the kitchen and spread her gaze out over the great hall. It was lit by candles and warmed by the hearth fire. She looked around at the faces filling the hall from the main entrance. Not just her kin but all the villagers and their children living within the walls of the stronghold. She loved living here with all of them, celebrating with people she loved and who loved her.

It was Hogmanay and feasts and merriment were underway. Quail pottage had been prepared by her and the other women in her family, along with crannachan, made with fresh raspberries, honey, and whisky. There was crowdie cheese and oats, basil salmon pâté and spinach tarts, not including various other dishes and desserts.

She'd helped dress the tables in white ribbon and green laurel. She'd placed candles with care inside wreaths made of pine and their cones. Everyone had a place. Everyone had a seat. Her handsome Uncle Nicky and his wife, Julianna, made sure of it.

Elysande's gaze swept to the table where the three brothers usually sat with their wives. Uncle Torin and his wife hadn't yet arrived. She knew the stories of her uncles' pasts, how the English tore their family apart when they were young children and set each on a different path.

She knew her father grew up on the battlefield, Uncle Torin had grown up alone and fighting for his life every day, and Uncle Nicky was a servant with no voice and no kin. She knew what the brothers had endured. But they rose high above it and helped turn the tides of the war for independence in King Robert's favor.

She wanted them to have peace. They deserved it.

She searched the other tables, but Raphael hadn't yet arrived.

The aroma of hens and capercallies roasting and various bread puddings baking permeated the air and filled Elysande's head with thoughts of eating. She'd been cooking and baking with her kin all day. Now was time to enjoy the fruit of her labors.

She pulled off her apron and smoothed out any wrinkles in her green skirts and embroidered kirtle.

It was going to be a night of celebrations, including the traditional first-footing. They would all visit their neighbor's home. It boded well if a tall, dark man was the first to cross one's threshold after midnight.

Elysande was certain many households wanted Raphael to be the first to visit.

She found him entering the hall and yanked off her baking bonnet. She patted her soft waves and she sized him up, admiring him from across the distance. He wore a loose léine, open at the collar. It had billowing sleeves that reached his long, broad fingers. He wore a black and green, short, sleeveless tunic belted at the waist. Elysande's grandmother, Berengaria, crafted the tunic.

He took a step toward her, as if he could not defy the temptation. His muscular legs were encased in snug, black hose and boots that reached his calves.

Elysande wanted to run her hands over him and feel the steel from which he was crafted.

He was intercepted by her cousins, Elias, Galeren, Joel, and Robin. They didn't go to him in anger but in friendship and with laughter and drinks.

"He has been accepted into the fold," Uncle Torin said, appearing beside her, watching with her. "There will be peace at last."

Elysande smiled and felt the sting of tears behind her eyes. Apparently, Raphael's father asked forgiveness for killing Amish MacRae, her father's friend. There was a bit of trouble for a little while about Adam the shepherd who led them out of the storm and into the cottage and warmth. There were seven shepherds who lived just outside the stronghold, guarding the sheep. None of them were called Adam. None of them matched the description Raphael gave.

Father Timothy and Brother Simon believed Adam was an angel, sent to save Elysande. Her father and others were a bit more skeptical until grandmother Berengaria claimed to have seen Adam twice. One of those times was Christmas day when she saw him inside the stronghold.

When questioned about what she knew of him, she shrugged her delicate shoulders and replied, "He comes and he goes."

Elysande greeted Aunt Braya when she approached, looking like a radiant angel in a pale coral gown and her hair pinned up above her head like a bright halo. Elysande smiled when her uncle dipped his wife backward and kissed her.

"Ye enter a room and I can breathe again," he told her as he escorted her to her chair.

Elysande sighed as they took their seats and leaned closer to each other to speak more intimately.

She would have such romance with Raphael! Tonight, she would tell her father.

He hadn't said whether he believed Raphael about the angel or not, but he told everyone what Raphael had done for her and for his father. He would accept a peace treaty with the Camerons but he still didn't want her spending too much time with Cameron's son.

She had never defied her father before, but she spent as much time with Raphael as possible. They snuck off together many times during the twelve days he and his father were here. They kissed and laughed and kissed some more. They spoke about a future together and even planned a family. Elysande felt as if she'd known Raphael for years instead of days. She wanted no one but him as a husband. She wanted her betrothal to Hugh Tanner broken and she wanted her father's blessing when she became a Cameron. She knew it was a lot to ask. But she would marry Raphael with or without her father's support. She would prefer to have it.

Suddenly, there was a flutter of giggles around her. Adela and her younger sister, Geva, along with other gels from the village. Their giggles had to do with Raphael, of course. His slow, confident gait oozed strength and sensuality. How would she tell them all that Raphael was hers?

Her eyes cut away from the girls as if with a will of their own to him, trying politely to break free of her cousins and get to her. She giggled that this was what their life would be like, filled with family.

Her father stood up from his seat and held up his arm for silence.

Elysande's heart pounded hard in her chest. Her feet began moving, taking her to her cousins' table. Raphael met her there and they shared a bold smile. She turned to her cousin, Elias, and caught the wink he tossed her. She had told him about loving Raphael and telling her father. He promised to stand with her and urged her not to fear.

"There is somethin' I wish to say this night," her father began. "To my family. To my friends. First to my brothers." He looked down at them and raised his cup of warm wassail. "My entire childhood was spent prayin' to find ye both. It didna happen until we were men, hardened by life and by the world. We lived through much—but here we are, together, a family. With us are our wives, strong determined women who sought our hearts in the wasteland and pulled us back to life." He lifted his cup and the people cheered again. He spoke to Father Timothy, his loyal and truest friend, Brother Simon, who burst from his spot at the table and ran, terrified at the cat under his chair.

Elias rose from his chair right away to rescue the cat from the howling man.

People laughed and, finally, when Elias held the cat securely, so did Brother Simon.

"I want to let ye all know that Robbie Cameron and I signed the treaty of peace between us." More cheering. Then, "I'm thankful fer ye all," he continued. "I'm thankful that my brother and I found one another. I'm thankful fer a good, loyal, lovin', beautiful wife who can set me flat on my arse when she wants to!"

Everyone laughed.

"I'm thankful fer my friends, old and new. And mostly, I'm thankful fer my children—all our children. They will do better things than we did.

"And lastly, I'm thankful that God brought a man of courage and integrity here to the stronghold."

He set his sapphire eyes on Raphael and Elysande's heart quaked so hard she was sure everyone could hear it.

"I revoke my daughter's betrothal to Hugh Tanner and offer her hand, if she wishes, to Raphael Cameron."

For a moment, Elysande just stared at him, and then at Raphael, and then at Hugh—who must have known about this because of his lowered gaze and silent tongue.

"D'ye wish it?"

"Aye!" She wasn't sure whom she answered, but she said it loud enough for everyone's ears. She leaped into Raphael's arms and let him kiss her face. Her father gave his blessing! Not only for her to marry, but for her to marry a Cameron!

Truly, it was a miracle.

She looked up with a heart filled with thanks, and then she laughed when all her cousins and friends swallowed her and Raphael up in their arms to congratulate her.

She had everything she could ever desire right here in the great hall of the even greater MacPherson stronghold.

The End

About the Author

Paula Quinn is a New York Times bestselling author and a sappy romantic moved by music, beautiful words, and the sight of a really nice pen. She lives in New York with her three beautiful children, six over-protective chihuahuas, and three adorable parrots. She loves to read romance and science fiction and has been writing since she was eleven. She's a faithful believer in God and thanks Him daily for all the blessings in her life. She loves all things medieval, but it is her love for Scotland that pulls at her heartstrings.

To date, four of her books have garnered Starred reviews from Publishers Weekly. She has been nominated as Historical Storyteller of the Year by RT Book Reviews, and all the books in her MacGregor and Children of the Mist series have received Top Picks from RT Book Reviews. Her work has also been honored as Amazons Best of the Year in Romance, and in 2008 she won the Gayle Wilson Award of Excellence for Historical Romance.

Website:

pa0854.wixsite.com/paulaquinn

Printed in Great Britain
by Amazon